S0-BNR-633

The Tale of
Two Bad Mice

The Tale of
Two Bad Mice

by Beatrix Potter

DERRYDALE BOOKS

New York

ONCE upon a time there was a very beautiful doll's house; it was red brick with white windows, and it had real cotton curtains and a front door and a chimney.

It belonged to two Dolls
called Lucinda and Jane; at
least it belonged to Lucinda,
but she never ordered meals.

Jane was the Cook; but she
never did any cooking,
because the dinner had been
bought ready-made, in a box
full of shavings.

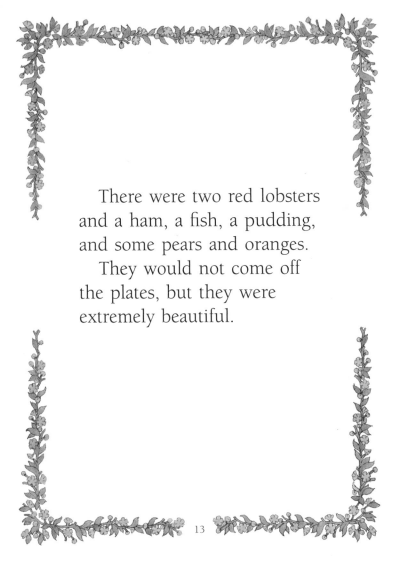

There were two red lobsters
and a ham, a fish, a pudding,
and some pears and oranges.
They would not come off
the plates, but they were
extremely beautiful.

One morning Lucinda and Jane had gone out for a drive in the doll's carriage. There was no one in the nursery, and it was very quiet. Presently there was a little scuffling, scratching noise in a corner near the fireplace, where there was a hole under the baseboard.

Tom Thumb put out his head for a moment, and then popped it in again.

Tom Thumb was a mouse.

A minute afterwards, Hunca
Munca, his wife, put her head
out, too; and when she saw
that there was no one in the
nursery, she ventured out on
the oilcloth under the coal
box.

The doll's house stood at
the other side of the fireplace.
Tom Thumb and Hunca
Munca went cautiously across
the hearthrug. They pushed
the front door—it was not
fast.

Tom Thumb and Hunca Munca went upstairs and peeped into the dining room. Then they squeaked with joy!

Such a lovely dinner was laid out upon the table! There were tin spoons, and lead knives and forks, and two doll's chairs—all *so* convenient!

Tom Thumb set to work at once to carve the ham. It was a beautiful shiny yellow, streaked with red.

The knife crumpled up and hurt him; he put his finger in his mouth.

"It is not boiled enough; it is hard. You have a try, Hunca Munca."

Hunca Munca stood up in her chair, and chopped at the ham with another lead knife.

"It's as hard as the hams at the cheese store," said Hunca Munca.

The ham broke off the plate with a jerk, and rolled under the table.

"Let it alone," said Tom Thumb; "give me some fish, Hunca Munca!"

Hunca Munca tried every tin spoon in turn; the fish was glued to the dish.

Then Tom Thumb lost his temper. He put the ham in the middle of the floor, and hit it with the tongs and with the shovel—bang, bang, smash, smash!

The ham flew all into pieces, for underneath the shiny paint it was made of nothing but plaster!

Then there was no end to
the rage and disappointment
of Tom Thumb and Hunca
Munca. They broke up the
pudding, the lobsters, the
pears and the oranges.

As the fish would not come
off the plate, they put it into
the red-hot crinkly paper fire
in the kitchen; but it would
not burn either.

Tom Thumb went up the kitchen chimney and looked out at the top—there was no soot.

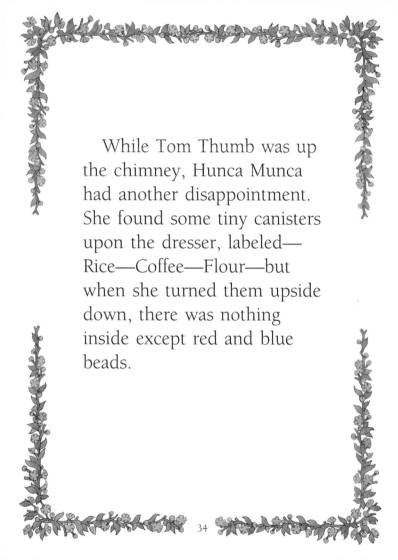

While Tom Thumb was up
the chimney, Hunca Munca
had another disappointment.
She found some tiny canisters
upon the dresser, labeled—
Rice—Coffee—Flour—but
when she turned them upside
down, there was nothing
inside except red and blue
beads.

Then those mice set to work to do all the mischief they could—especially Tom Thumb! He took Jane's clothes out of the chest of drawers in her bedroom, and he threw them out of the top floor window.

But Hunca Munca had a frugal mind. After pulling half the feathers out of Lucinda's pillow, she remembered that she herself was in want of a feather bed.

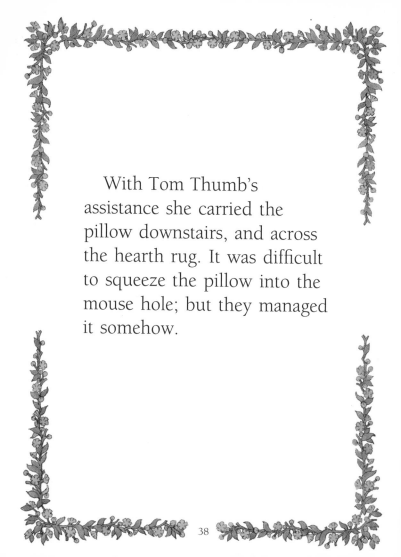

With Tom Thumb's
assistance she carried the
pillow downstairs, and across
the hearth rug. It was difficult
to squeeze the pillow into the
mouse hole; but they managed
it somehow.

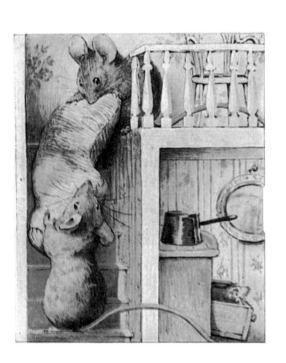

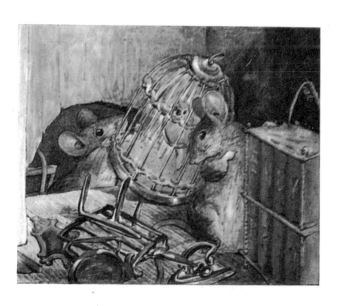

Then Hunca Munca went
back and fetched a chair, a
book case, a bird cage, and
several small odds and ends.
The book case and the bird
cage refused to go into the
mouse hole.

Hunca Munca left them
behind the coal box, and went
to fetch a cradle.

Hunca Munca was just
returning with another chair,
when suddenly there was a
noise of talking outside upon
the landing. The mice rushed
back to their hole, and the
dolls came into the nursery.

What a sight met the eyes of Jane and Lucinda! Lucinda sat upon the upset kitchen stove and stared; and Jane leant against the kitchen dresser and smiled—but neither of them made any remark.

The book case and the bird
cage were rescued from under
the coal box—but Hunca
Munca has got the cradle, and
some of Lucinda's clothes.

She also has some useful
pots and pans, and several
other things.

The little girl that the doll's house belonged to, said—"I will get a doll dressed like a policeman!"

But the nurse said—"I will set a mouse trap!"

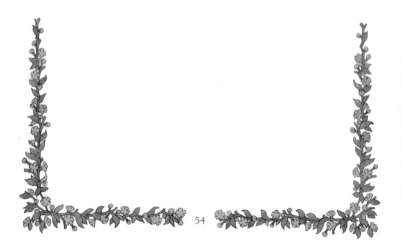

So that is the story of the two Bad Mice—but they were not so very very naughty after all, because Tom Thumb paid for everything he broke.

He found a crooked six-pence under the hearth rug; and on Christmas Eve, he and Hunca Munca stuffed it into one of the stockings of Lucinda and Jane.

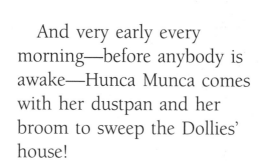

And very early every morning—before anybody is awake—Hunca Munca comes with her dustpan and her broom to sweep the Dollies' house!

THE END

ABOUT BEATRIX POTTER

Born in London in 1866, Beatrix Potter spent a lonely childhood. Her well-to-do parents did not send her to school, but instead had her taught by governesses at home. Her only friend was her younger brother Bertram. On vacations in Scotland, she and Bertram escaped into a world of farms, woods, and fields, where they delighted in watching and collecting plants, animals, and insects.

In London, yearning for the country, and the fascinating little animals she loved, Beatrix kept small pets in her nursery—a rabbit, some mice, snails, and even a hedgehog—and began to draw them, as well as plants and flowers she had seen in the countryside.

Out of these drawings grew her illustrated stories about rabbits and other small animals. They began as letters to children, then became published books. The stories were so popular that at the age of thirty-six, Beatrix Potter found herself a successful children's author. She continued to write and illustrate her delightful tales, eventually more than two dozen, and successive generations of children have cherished them.

Editorial Note

The language of Beatrix Potter's stories includes certain British words or phrases which may be unfamiliar to today's American children. Therefore, in a few cases, the text has been altered slightly to make it more comprehensible. The changes, however, have been kept to a minimum to retain the charm of the original.

Dedication

FOR
W. M. L. W.
THE LITTLE GIRL
WHO HAD THE DOLL'S HOUSE

"About Beatrix Potter"
Copyright © 1992 by Outlet Book Company, Inc.
All rights reserved.

This 1992 edition is published by Derrydale Books, distributed by
Outlet Book Company, Inc., a Random House Company,
225 Park Avenue South, New York, New York 10003.

Printed and bound in the United States of America

Library of Congress Cataloging-in-Publication Data

Potter, Beatrix, 1866–1943.
    The tale of two bad mice / by Beatrix Potter.
        p.   cm.
    Summary: While the dolls are away, two curious, naughty mice
explore the dolls' house and steal their furniture.
    ISBN 0–517–07241–6
    [1. Mice—Fiction.   2. Dollhouses—Fiction.]   I. Title.
PZ7.P85Tatc   1992
[E]—dc20   91–34155
                                                      CIP
                                                      AC

For this edition of The Tale of Two Bad Mice:
Cover and interior design: Clair Moritz
Production supervision: Helen Marra and Ellen Reed
Editorial supervision: Claire Booss

8   7   6   5   4   3   2   1